Published by Pleasant Company Publications
© 2003 Helen Craig Limited and Katharine Holabird

The Angelina Ballerina name and character and the dancing Angelina logo are trademarks of HIT Entertainment PLC,
Katharine Holabird, and Helen Craig. ANGELINA is registered in the U.K. and Japan.
The dancing Angelina logo is registered in the U.K.

Visit our Web site at **www.americangirl.com** and
Angelina's very own site at **www.angelinaballerina.com**

Printed in Malaysia.
03 04 05 06 07 08 09 10 TWP 10 9 8 7 6 5 4 3 2 1

Cataloging-in-Publication data available from the Library of Congress

Angelina Ballerina's
Invitation to the Ballet

Story by Katharine Holabird Illustrations by Helen Craig

One morning when Angelina skipped and hopped downstairs for breakfast, she found a large envelope waiting for her.

"Who could it be from?" Mrs. Mouseling asked with a smile.

Angelina recognized Miss Lilly's handwriting and couldn't wait to open the envelope.

Miss Angelina Mouseling
Vine Cottage
Huckleberry Lane
Chipping Cheddar
MOUSELAND

Lilly Mousakova, Dip. MRBS
Miss Lilly's Ballet School
The Village Green
Chipping Cheddar
Mouseland

Congratulations, Angelina,

You've won our ballet school charity raffle!

The prize is two tickets for the Gala

Performance of "Cindermouse" at

the Royal Ballet on June 24th.

Your favorite ballerina, Serena Silvertail,

will be the star!

With love and best wishes,

Miss Lilly

x x x x

"I can't believe it! I've won two tickets to see Serena Silvertail at the Royal Ballet this Friday!" Angelina was so excited, she pirouetted three times around the kitchen table.

"I'm going to invite Alice!" Angelina shouted as she flew out the door.

Angelina raced as fast as she could to Alice's house, but when she got there, Alice had already received a surprise of her own.

Miss Alice Nimbletoes
56 Corncob Road
Chipping Cheddar
Mouseland

Ssssh! It's Top Secret!

You are specially invited to

PRISCILLA and PENELOPE's

Birthday Party

Friday, June 24th,

2pm at the Grand Ballroom

Village Hall, Chipping Cheddar

ENTERTAINMENT BY

FAT-CAT the CLOWN

CATERING by
THE CHEESE WIZARD COMPANY
THE CHEDDAR SOUFFLE
ACORN SUPREME ICE CREAM
and the biggest, most delicious
PINK PASSION CHEESECAKE ever!

R.S.V.P Immediately to Mrs. Reginald Pink Paws
5 Primrose Hill, Chipping Cheddar

"The twins didn't invite me to
their stupid secret birthday!"
Angelina sniffed.
"But I don't care—I've
just won two tickets to the
Cindermouse ballet on Friday.
Will you come with me, Alice?"

"Oh, dear, Angelina," Alice groaned. "I wish I could,
but I just told the twins I'll be at their party."

"Oh, no!" cried Angelina.

"I'm very, very sorry," Alice whispered tearfully.

Angelina gave her best friend a hug. "I'll have
to go without you," she said bravely,
"but I'm sure William would love to
see Serena Silvertail dance."

Angelina waved good-bye and raced off to look for William. She found him down at Miller's Pond playing around with his boat.

"William, can you come with me to the Royal Ballet on Friday?" asked Angelina eagerly.

"Crumbs, Angelina," said William, shaking his head. "I promised to help Sammy on Friday."

William pulled a scruffy envelope out of his pocket and showed it to her.

WILLIAM LONG TAIL
RAILROAD CROSZING COTTAGE
CABBAGE Street
CHIPPING CHEDDAR
MOUSELAND

Hiya William!

It's yer old freind Sammy!
Wot about sum futbal with all
the gang?
We relly need anuther playere on
Fri. June 24th cos Spike's broke
his paw real bad so you better
come. Or else!
ha ha ha

Sammy
and His Terible Gang!

Angelina shrugged. "Well, at least there's always Henry," she sighed, and she went off to find her cousin at the village playground.

"Come and swing with me!" Henry cried when he saw Angelina.

But Angelina didn't feel like swinging. She showed Henry and Aunt Lavender the ballet tickets.

"Please, could Henry come with me?" Angelina asked.

"Oh, yes!" Henry shouted.

"What a pity," said Aunt Lavender. "Henry's got an appointment with Dr. Tuttle that afternoon."

Welcome to
CHIPPING
CHEDDAR
CLINIC

POSTAGE
PAID
MOUSELAND
TUESDAY
21st JUNE
9·00 a.m.

2

ROYAL MOUSE MAIL

Henry Mouseling

5 The Burrows

Chipping Cheddar

Mouseland

Dr. Tobias Tuttle MBBS, DRCOG, DCH
The Clinic • High Street • Chipping Cheddar • Mouseland

To: ....Henry Mouseling............

Your next appointment is on: Friday, June 24th, at 2 p.m.

Tooth and whisker examination and thorough cleaning.
Tail measurement. Paw and ear tests.

Don't forget:
Mouselings need strong teeth, so don't eat too many sweeties.

Signed, your friend,

Dr. T. Tuttle

Angelina's tail drooped as she walked home sadly.
She didn't want to go to the *Cindermouse* ballet
without a friend, but who else could she invite?

Just then Miss Lilly came rushing down the street.

"I've been looking everywhere for you, Angelina!" Miss Lilly exclaimed.
"Something quite extraordinary has happened." She handed Angelina a letter.

Miss Lilly Mousakova, Dip. MRBS

Miss Lilly's Ballet School

The Village Green

Chipping Cheddar

Mouseland

Ivor Operatski, Director
The Mouseland Royal Ballet Company
Edamville, Mouseland

My dearest Lilly,

Please help an old friend at the Royal Ballet!
This Friday we will be performing our Royal Gala
"Cindermouse" ballet with Serena Silvertail, but, alas, one
of our little ballerinas took a tumble in rehearsal and
fractured her tail!

I understand that one of your students, Miss Angelina
Mouseling, is a remarkable dancer. We urgently need her
to join our production – rehearsals have begun. She must
be on the express train to Edamville first thing tomorrow.

Don't let me down, my dearest Lilly!

Ivor

P.S. I've enclosed a Royal Ballet poster signed by
Serena Silvertail for Angelina.

"What do you think, Angelina?" asked Miss Lilly. "Would you like to dance at the Royal Ballet?"

Angelina was already jumping up and down. "I can't wait!" she cried.

Mr. and Mrs. Mouseling were absolutely amazed when they saw Mr. Operatski's letter.

"And now I can invite you to the ballet!" said Angelina as she proudly gave her parents the two tickets.

"We wouldn't miss this show for anything," said Mrs. Mouseling.

The next day when Angelina arrived at the Royal Ballet, she immediately began rehearsing the Cindermouse Waltz. She had to work very hard to learn all of the steps.

Before she knew it, it was time for the Gala Performance. Angelina began to feel nervous. After all, she was about to dance with the best ballerina in Mouseland!

Just then, Mr. Operatski dashed into the dressing room. "This arrived for you," he said, handing Angelina an envelope.

1st Class Mail

Miss Angelina Mouseling
The Royal Ballet School
15 Queen Seraphina Square
EDAMVILLE
Mouseland

After reading the lovely card from her parents, Angelina felt much braver. "I'm ready!" she called as she twirled out the door of the dressing room.

As Angelina waltzed onstage at Cindermouse's ball, her costume sparkled in the spotlight. Dancing with Serena Silvertail was so exciting that Angelina forgot to be nervous—in fact, she loved every minute.

"This has been the most exciting day of my life," Angelina sighed as she snuggled into her mother's lap on the train ride home. "I must be the luckiest mouseling in all of Mouseland!"

Then Angelina yawned two huge yawns, and soon she was fast asleep, dreaming of dancing at the Royal Ballet.